Pat a Pan

Written by Catherine Baker
Illustrated by Melanie Mitchell

Collins

a pan

a tin

tap tap

pat pat

tap it

6

pat it

tip it

pat it

a tin

tap tap tap

a pan

tip it in

/a/

14

After reading

Letters and Sounds: Phase 2

Word count: 26

Focus phonemes: /a/ /t/ /p/ /i/ /n/

Curriculum links: Understanding the World: The World

Early learning goals: Reading: Use phonic knowledge to decode regular words and read them aloud accurately; demonstrate understanding when talking with others about what they have read

Developing fluency

- Encourage your child to sound talk and then blend the words, e.g. p/a/n. It may help to point to each sound as your child reads.
- Then ask your child to reread each page to support fluency and understanding.
- You could reread the whole book to your child to model fluency.

Phonic practice

- Ask your child to sound talk and blend each of the following words: t/a/p, t/i/p, p/a/t, p/a/n.
- Can you point to the words that have a /p/ sound in them? (*pan, pat, tip, tap*)
- Look at the "I spy sounds" pages (14–15). Discuss the picture with your child. Can they find items/examples of words with the /a/ sound? (*athlete, axe, anorak, ant, anteater, apples, anchor, fan, bag, hat, tap, pan*)

Extending vocabulary

- Ask your child:
  o The child taps the pan. What other words can we use instead of **tap**? (e.g. *hit, bang, bash, knock, pat, thump*)
  o Look at page 10. The children are tapping the tin. What sound do you think it would make? (e.g. *bang, ting, ring, ping, clang*)
  o Look through the book. What different types of containers can you see? Can you think of any others? (e.g. *bowl, box, tin, tray, jug, watering can*)